ROCK-A-BYE BABY

AND MORE BEDTIME RHYMES

ILLUSTRATED BY

KRISTA BRAUCKMANN–TOWNS

WENDY EDELSON

ANITA NELSON

LORI NELSON FIELD

DEBBIE PINKNEY

KAREN PRITCHETT

NEW SEASONS

PUBLISHING

Wee Willie Winkie

Wee Willie Winkie
  Runs through the town,
Upstairs and downstairs
  In his nightgown,
Rapping at the window,
  Crying through the lock,
Are the children all in bed?
  Now it's eight o'clock.

Sleep, Baby, Sleep

Sleep, baby, sleep.
  Your father guards the sheep
Your mother shakes
  The dreamland tree,
And from it fall
  Sweet dreams for thee.
Sleep, baby, sleep.

Rock-a-Bye, Baby

Rock-a-bye, baby,
  On the treetop.
When the wind blows,
  The cradle will rock.
When the bough breaks,
  The cradle will fall.
Down will come baby,
  Cradle and all.

Hush-a-Bye

Hush-a-bye, baby,
  Lie still with your daddy.
Your mommy has gone to the mill,
  To get some meal to bake a cake.
So please, my dear baby, lie still.

Sleep Tight

Good night,
Sleep tight,
Don't let the
bedbugs bite.

The Cock Crows

The cock crows in the morn
  To tell us to rise,
And he that lies late
  Will never be wise:
For early to bed
  And early to rise
Is the way to be healthy
  And wealthy and wise.

Come, Let's to Bed

Come, let's to bed,
Says Sleepy-head.
Sit up awhile, says Slow.

Hang on the pot,
  Says Greedy-gut,
We'll sup before we go.

To bed, to bed,
  Cried Sleepy-head,
But all the rest said no!

It is morning now;
  You must milk the cow,
And tomorrow to bed we go.

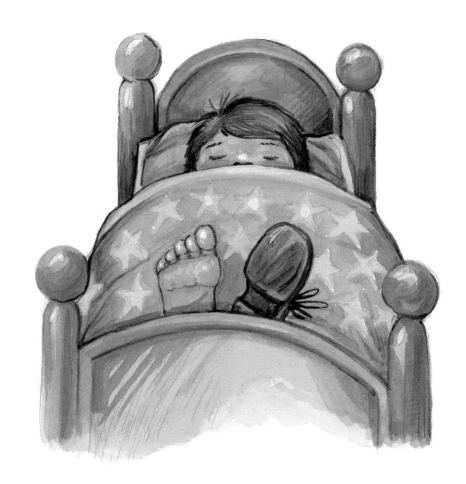

Diddle, Diddle, Dumpling

Diddle, diddle, dumpling,
  My son John,
Went to bed with his trousers on;
  One shoe off, and one shoe on,
Diddle, diddle, dumpling,
  My son John.

Sleepy Cat

The cat sat asleep
  By the side of the fire.
The mistress snored loud as a pig.

John took up his fiddle,
  By Jenny's desire,
And struck up a bit of a jig.